MICK HARTE

WAS HERE

Favorites by Barbara Park

PICTURE BOOKS
Ma! There's Nothing to Do Here!
Psssst! It's Me . . . the Bogeyman

CHAPTER BOOKS
The Junie B. Jones series

MIDDLE-GRADE NOVELS

Almost Starring Skinnybones
Don't Make Me Smile
The Geek Chronicles 1: Maxie, Rosie,
and Earl—Partners in Grime
The Geek Chronicles 2: Rosie Swanson: Fourth-Grade
Geek for President
The Geek Chronicles 3: Dear God, Help!!! Love, Earl
The Graduation of Jake Moon
The Kid in the Red Jacket
Mick Harte Was Here
My Mother Got Married (and Other Disasters)
Operation: Dump the Chump
Skinnybones

MICK HARTE WAS HERE

Barbara Park

A Yearling Book

All rights reserved. Published in the United States by Yearling, an imprint of Random House Children's Books, a division of Penguin Random House LLC, New York. Originally published in hardcover in the United States by Alfred A. Knopf, an imprint of Random House Children's Books, New York, in 1995.

Yearling and the jumping horse design are registered trademarks of Penguin Random House LLC.

Visit us on the Web!
randomhousekids.com

Educators and librarians, for a variety of teaching tools, visit us at
RHTeachersLibrarians.com

Library of Congress Cataloging-in-Publication Data is available upon request.
ISBN 978-0-679-88203-9 (pbk.) — ISBN 978-1-5247-1827-5 (lib. bdg.)
ISBN 978-0-307-78682-1 (ebook)

Printed in the United States of America

49 48 47 46 45 44 43 42 41 40

First Yearling Edition 2006

*This is dedicated to all of those who are
happily tap dancing on God's piano.*

*A special thanks to my friend and editor, Anne Schwartz,
for her thoughtful insights and suggestions.*

Contents

Mick

) ust let me say right off the bat, it was a bike
   accident.

It was about as "accidental" as you can get,
too.

Like Mick wasn't riding crazy. Or dodging
in and out of traffic. And both of his hands
were on the handlebars and all like that.

His tire just hit a rock. And he skidded into
the back of a passing truck. And that was that.
There wasn't a scratch on him. It was a head
injury. Period.

So this isn't the kind of book where you meet the main character and you get to like him real well and then he dies at the end. I hate those kind of books. And besides, I can't think of anything worse than using my brother's accident as the tear-jerking climax to some tragic story.

I don't want to make you cry.

I just want to tell you about Mick.

But I thought you should know right up front that he's not here anymore.

I just thought that would be fair.

I'm only ten months older than he was.

I was "planned."

Mick was a surprise.

He loved it, too. Being a surprise, I mean. He was always teasing my parents about it. Telling them that even before he *existed,* he could outsmart two chemistry majors with birth control pills.

"Just imagine the amazing stunts I'll pull when I'm a sneaky, rebellious *teenager,*" he'd say. Then he'd rub his hands together and throw his head way back and do that kind of creepy laugh that mad scientists do in the movies. You know, like "Muuwhaaaahahahahaha . . ." and he'd hunch over and limp out of the room like Igor or somebody.

Mick was excellent at imitating voices, by the way. We have a tape of him yelling "I'm melting! I'm melting!" that sounds just like the Wicked Witch of the West in *The Wizard of Oz. Exactly,* I mean.

But even without playing the tape, I can still remember how he sounded. I've heard that sometimes when people you love die, you forget their voices. But I haven't forgotten Mick's. Not yet, anyway.

I have a weird kind of memory, I think. Like I've never once been able to remember my parents' anniversary in time to buy them a card. But I can still remember the exact conversation I had with Santa Claus when I was in kindergarten.

He said, "Ho ho ho."

I said, "Your breath smells."

And he said, "Get down."

It wasn't much of a chat, but the point is, it happened eight years ago and I still remember it like it was yesterday. That's why it doesn't surprise me that I can remember everything about the fight Mick and I had four weeks ago. On the morning of the accident.

It started out like most any other school day at our house. My father was running around wearing his usual morning outfit—a shirt and tie, boxer shorts, and black socks. It's pretty humiliating being related to a man in a get-up like that. But Pop never puts on his pants till right before he leaves for the office. He doesn't like to "ruin the crease" before he has to, he says. I'm serious.

My mother had already left for work, wearing her usual pair of jeans. But don't think the jeans mean she's more laid back than Pop. All they mean is that she works at a research lab doing experiments with viruses, and she doesn't like to spill germs on her good clothes.

Both of my parents are totally different from Mick and me. They're real methodical and

4

organized, and everything they do is always technically planned out. Like my mom never makes hamburgers for dinner without weighing out precise quarter-pound servings on her kitchen scale. And Pop's idea of a daring adventure is to wash his socks without pinning them to their mates.

Also, I've got name tags sewn into my underwear and I've never been to camp—which is downright disturbing, when you think about it.

On top of all that, my parents hate family conflict worse than any parents I've ever seen. Like my brother and I could hardly even raise our voices at each other before we'd be hustled off to our rooms to think about how we could "resolve our differences in a more civilized and resourceful manner."

Last year, my mother even made a schedule for me and Mick to follow on school mornings so we could all start the day without "confrontation." It was pretty simple, actually. Mick got the bathroom for twenty minutes while I ate breakfast. Then a timer would go off and we'd switch rooms.

At least we were *supposed* to switch rooms. But every so often, one of us would run late and we'd find ourselves in the same room at the same time. When that happened, we almost always ended up fighting. 'Cause I mean my parents did sort of expect it of us and all. And we really hated to disappoint them.

That's why—when Mick walked into the kitchen that morning and saw me digging around in the cereal box—he couldn't wait to get something started.

The first thing he did was try to grab the box away from me. "What's in there? What're you looking for? Lemme see," he said.

I held on as tight as I could and turned my back to him. "No! Get away! Get outta here!" I yelled.

I couldn't see what he was doing behind me. Couldn't hear him, either. Which worried me a lot. Because Mick was always at his most dangerous when he was quiet.

Then suddenly, out of nowhere, he came bounding off a kitchen chair and snatched the box right out of my hands.

"Hey! Give that back! I mean it, Mick! That tattoo is mine!"

As soon as I said the word "tattoo," his eyes opened real wide and he grinned this stupid grin of his. Then he reached right in and pulled it out. No trouble at all.

He dangled it in front of my face. It was one of those ugly skull-and-crossbones pirate tattoos.

I should probably mention that I didn't really *want* the tattoo. But that wasn't the point. The point was, I didn't want *him* to have it. Which I happen to think is a perfectly legitimate reason for fighting.

It just wasn't fair, that's all. Mick almost always got to the cereal toys before me. Then he'd hide them in his room and pretend he didn't know a thing about them. But I know for a fact he had at least five Super Balls and two pairs of 3-D glasses hidden in there somewhere.

"Come on, Mick! I want that tattoo! Hand it over!"

"Say 'please.'"

"Please, okay? Now let me have it!"

He tapped his chin. "Gee, I don't know, Phoeb. I hate to be picky, but your 'please' wasn't all that polite. Why don't you try it again. Only this time, say 'Pretty please with sugar on top.' "

I swear I could not believe he was doing this to me.

"Pretty please with sugar on top. Now give it!"

But even before I finished, Mick was already shaking his head again. "Nope. Sorry, but it's still not working for me. Maybe we should try something different this time. How 'bout this? . . . Try 'Wee Willie Winkie went to town. Upstairs, downstairs in his nightgown.' "

That's when I jumped on top of him and wrestled him to the ground. (I realize I'm too old to do stuff like that. But I'm not that bad a wrestler and I'm not quite ready to give it up.)

Anyhow, I almost had Mick in a headlock when my father walked in on us. Men who walk around in boxer shorts and socks are deceptively quiet, by the way.

He didn't yell. Pop almost never yells. Instead, he just folded his arms and gave us one of those "looks" of his. This was the one where he rolls his eyeballs so far back in his head he can see his brain, probably. Then he heaves this huge sigh—like having two children who fight over a press-on tattoo is a hardship too great for any human being to bear.

Trying to save his own skin, Mick jumped right up. "Here, Pop! Quick! Take this! Phoebe wanted it for herself, but I thought you might want to wear it to the office today."

He tried to press it to my father's wrist. But it wouldn't stick to the hair. So he just kept slapping at it.

"Boy, they sure don't make tattoos like they did when you were a young lad, do they, Pop?"

My father knew Mick was only joking around, but he didn't lighten up or anything. He just pointed his finger, first in my face and then in Mick's, and squinted his eyes in this silent threat thing he does.

Then, with the tattoo still hanging off his hand, he swiveled on his sock feet and padded back out of the kitchen.

"Yeah, but wait, Pop!" I called. "That tattoo was mine! All I was doing was getting it out of the box and Mick jumped on me!"

My father kept going.

"Can I please have it back? Please?"

Pop's bedroom door slammed.

I was steaming mad. Really fuming. But instead of backing off and letting me calm down, Mick started teasing me in this stupid pirate voice, saying stuff like "Shiver me timbers" and "Thar she blows," totally cracking himself up.

That's when I shoved him into the refrigerator and called him a name that I'd never called anybody before in my whole life.

A really ugly name, I mean. A street word that you mostly hear only on HBO, or on school playgrounds.

It shocked him that I said it.

It shocked me, too.

But instead of apologizing, I just turned my mouth up in this nasty little grin.

Mick pushed me away from him. Hard.

"You're cool, Phoebe," he said.

Then he walked out of the room.

That was our last morning together.

The last one ever, I mean.

It kills me when I remember that. Because usually I hardly cuss at all. At least not as much as most kids my age, I don't think. Mick didn't either. Which is almost *weird* for a seventh-grade boy.

Not that the two of us were angels or anything. I'm not saying that. We were always getting in trouble. But normally it was for stuff we did together. As a team. Because even though it sounds corny and all, when we weren't fighting, my brother and I actually *liked* each other. A lot.

I think it was the result of being so close in age. Like when Mick was learning to talk, I was the only one who could understand him, so I sort of became his translator. I mean right from the beginning I knew that *truck* meant dog, and that *meme-fluzit* meant he wanted to flush the toilet.

The first big "caper" we pulled together was right after Mick started kindergarten. That was when we defaced our first property. To be specific, we scratched the letters F-A-R-T in the new driveway that had just been poured next to our house.

We didn't do it to be bad. It's just that I was learning how to spell. And Mick was learning how to print. And the cement just sort of *called* to us, I guess you'd say.

Mick promised that if I would tell him the right letters, he'd do a good job with his printing. He did, too. I mean his R was backward, but at the time neither of us knew the difference.

All I remember is how excited we both were when he finished. We clapped, and jumped up and down, and totally laughed our heads off. Without a doubt, this was the funniest thing anyone had ever done in the entire history of the universe.

It's amazing how a little fart in the driveway can totally lose its humor when your father sees it.

I really don't want to go into all the details of what happened when he discovered it that night. But I will tell you that when he and Mom stood us in front of them and made us "solemnly swear" to tell them the "complete and honest truth" about how it got there, Mick swallowed hard, took a big step forward, and told them "a monkey did it."

Seriously. He said that.

The trouble was, I had to back him up on it. I didn't really have a choice, you know? So I stood there and swore that we had both seen a monkey run into the driveway with a little stick in his hand and write "fart" in the concrete.

Then—just to make the story even *more* believable—Mick said the monkey's name was Zippy. And the two of us had saved the day by chasing him "all the way back to Africa."

We ended up going to our rooms for a week or something, I think. But after a while, it became one of those things that everyone looks back on and laughs about.

Like even on the morning of the fight, when I went out the door and saw that backward R in the cement, I smiled a little bit. I didn't want to. But I did.

Sirens

I walk to school with my best friend, Zoe Santos. In elementary school we used to ride our bikes. But mine's pink. With a white basket. Which was fine in fourth grade, but I figure my teen years are going to be hard enough without being seen around town on a bike that Little Bo Peep would have picked.

Mick didn't have that problem. His bike was black and chrome—which is why he could still ride it to school and not look like a complete doofus.

Not looking like a doofus was pretty important to Mick, actually. It's not that he was conceited. It's just that when he was eight, my mother made the mistake of showing him his christening gown, and he never really got over it.

I mean who could blame him? It was this long, lacy white thing with blue ribbons and a matching lace hat.

He had a fit when he saw it. "But that's a dress!" he shouted. "You mean you took me to church in a dress? And people saw me in it? And they knew I was a *guy*?"

My mother explained about how it wasn't really a dress. It was a gown. The same gown my father had worn. And my grandfather, too. But nothing helped. For the rest of the year, the only thing Mick would wear to Sunday school without a battle was a black T-shirt with a motorcycle on the front of it, and the kind of camouflage pants that Marines wear.

They were neatly pressed, though. In this ridiculous compromise with my father, Mick agreed to let Pop iron creases down the pant legs.

Anyway, it didn't take long before it was the only outfit he'd wear to school, too. Which sounds extreme and all. But the school psychologist told my mother it was Mick's way of balancing out the "trauma of being paraded around in public wearing ladies' sleepwear."

By fourth grade he'd finally gotten over his obsession with "macho" clothes and he became "trendy" instead. In fact, he got so picky about what he wore, my parents would actually flip a coin to see who had to take him to buy school clothes. The first time my father lost the toss, he came home from his day at the mall with some of his hair pulled out.

Still, even Pop had to admit that Mick was a sharp dresser. A lot of girls had crushes on him. But other than me, the only girl he hung around with was Zoe. They really liked each other, too. Not like boyfriend and girlfriend, I don't mean. But they both had naturally curly hair, and they both thought professional wrestling was real—which are two pretty strong bonds, when you think about it.

Anyhow, that's why Zoe was a little hurt

when Mick passed us on his bike that morning and he didn't say hi to her.

"It's not you he's mad at. It's me," I said. "We just had a fight and I called him a bad name."

"What bad name?"

I didn't want to tell her, but she wouldn't stop looking at me.

"Okay, okay. It's the word that comedian kept saying on that HBO special we promised your mother we wouldn't watch the other night."

You could almost see Zoe's mind clicking down the choices. But as soon as she hit on the right one, she just shrugged it off. Cuss words don't impress Zoe one way or the other.

"He'll be over it by lunch," she said.

I knew she was probably right. No matter how hard he tried, Mick could never stay mad at me. Like even at his most furious, the longest he could last was a couple of hours.

That's why I wasn't surprised when he came running up behind me as I was walking out of the cafeteria that day.

"Hey, Phoeb! Wait up! I need you to do me a favor, okay? I need you to ride my bike home from school. Dillon Rigby's mother is taking a bunch of us to his house so we can rehearse the announcement for Friday's basketball game. He's got one of those Mr. Microphone things."

He tossed me the key to his bike lock.

I tossed it back. "Sorry. I've got soccer practice after school. Plus I've got a ton of books to carry home tonight."

He looked at Zoe, but she was already walking away. "Can't do it either, Mick. If I don't take my science project home this afternoon, Mr. Garcia's going to drop me a whole grade. He says it's starting to stink up the science wing."

Mick rolled his eyes. "Great. Wonderful. Now I have to ride over there all by myself and I don't even know where the kid lives."

"Aaah, no big deal. You'll be fine," I said, casual as anything.

Then I just walked away.

I didn't even say goodbye.

I'm running sprints at soccer practice when I hear the siren. I stop right away and stretch my neck to see if an ambulance is coming.

It bothers me that I'm kind of hypnotized by the sight of an ambulance. I don't want to be one of those creeps who gawk at accident scenes. But I am, I think. Because as soon as I see the flashing red light appear over the fence, I can't take my eyes off it. And so like always, I just cover my ears and watch it come.

The ambulance is getting close to the soccer field now. But instead of speeding past, it seems to be slowing down. Then it slows even more and turns the corner in front of the building.

My stomach starts to churn. I don't like having the ambulance turn there. By now it should be speeding off to someone else's neighborhood. A neighborhood where I don't know anyone.

But even after another minute or two, the noise of the siren hasn't faded at all. And with my ears still covered, I walk to the sidelines and sit down in the grass. "Just turn the damn thing off!" I scream inside my head.

Then they do. But the noise it makes as it winds down is worse than the siren itself. And I can't understand how some of the girls on my team have already started running sprints again.

Then all of a sudden, the door of the gym flies open and one of the school secretaries comes rushing out. The old one. Only she's moving pretty fast—sprinting practically—over to my coach.

A few seconds later, Coach Brodie is running full speed in my direction.

I've replayed that scene in my head a hundred times since the day it happened.

But every single time I get to the part where Coach Brodie's arms go around me, my muscles still tense just like they did that afternoon.

"Phoebe, honey. It's Mick," she says.

And for the second time that day, I am shocked by what comes out of my mouth.

I say, "I know."

Thinking back, I'm not exactly clear what happened after that. It's sort of like the film in my mind speeds up and there's just a blur of people walking me to the office. And bits and pieces of conversation. Mick's name. The name of the hospital. Talk about how fast the ambulance got there.

And it's strange, you know? Because the only thing that I really *do* remember is the feeling that none of it was really happening. It's more like it was a play or something, and I was acting out a role. Like, "The part of the victim's sister is being played by Phoebe Harte."

So I sat in the principal's chair. And I sipped at the water the nurse gave me. And I let people smooth my hair.

And I remember thinking how weird it was that instead of crying, I kept focusing on stupid stuff. Like how the nurse's zipper was halfway down. And how the principal, Mrs. Berryhill, could use a Tic Tac.

Even when Zoe and her mother came into the office to take me home, I didn't fall apart or anything. I didn't even stand up right away. I just sat and waited until Mrs. Santos had finished signing me out. Then, calm as anything, I followed her and Zoe out to their car.

The Santoses live across the street from me. So when Mrs. Santos took a left out of the parking lot, instead of a right toward home, a signal went off in my brain that we were going in the

21

wrong direction. And I automatically turned and looked out the back window.

That's when I saw it.

The truck, I mean.

And Mick's bike.

Still lying in the gutter where he had fallen.

I remember making a noise then. This awful noise that didn't sound like me at all—but like one of those old women that you see on the news sometimes. One of those crying old women at the scene of some terrible natural disaster.

Zoe's arms went around me. But when she tried to talk, her voice was shaky and it kept breaking. "Oh God, Phoebe. Please don't cry. Everything is going to be okay. I swear it is."

I pushed her away.

"Stop it," I said.

It sounds mean. I know it does. But the idea that anyone could comfort me was almost insulting, if you want to know the truth.

My brother's bike was in the gutter. And I didn't want to be hugged. Or held. Or even touched for that matter.

I just wanted for it not to be Mick.

So I closed my eyes, and I did the only thing I could.

I prayed to God that it was all a terrible mistake and Mick hadn't been the one riding it.

I prayed it had been one of his friends.

I'm sorry for that. I swear I am.

But still, that was my prayer.

When we got to Zoe's house, there was a message on the answering machine from Pop. He told Mrs. Santos to keep me there until he came. That's when I was forced to face the fact that it was really Mick who had been hurt, and right away I started begging Mrs. Santos to take me to the hospital.

She didn't give in, though. She was nice about it. But she didn't give in. So finally I went to Zoe's room, climbed up onto the top of her bunk bed, and started praying like crazy. Ordering God to make my brother okay.

I couldn't lie still. Even while I was praying, I kept tossing and turning and looking down at the clock on Zoe's dresser. One time my arm dangled over the side of the bed, and Zoe reached up from the bottom bunk and held on to my fingers.

It almost made me cry when she did that.

Mrs. Santos tiptoed into the room a few times, bringing stuff to eat. I told her I wasn't hungry. But I don't think my hunger had much to do with why she kept on fixing food. Grating cheese for nachos just helped make the time go by for her, I think.

After her third trip, I remember looking over the edge of the bunk to see what all she had brought in. Besides the nachos, there was a pitcher of lemonade, chips and homemade salsa, four blueberry muffins, a bunch of grapes, and a package of Ho Hos.

I'm not kidding. It was like a meal that Henry VIII would eat or something. Henry VIII was that big fat glutton king of England with all the wives. You've probably seen actors playing him on TV. He's almost always shown gnawing on a turkey leg or with a slab of roast beef hanging out of his mouth or something.

I wouldn't be such an expert on him, but Mick was Henry VIII for Halloween in fifth grade. That was the year he attached his beard with superglue and ended up wearing it to school for a week.

Mick always dressed up as people you'd never think of in a million years. Like in sixth grade he went as Clarence Birdseye, the father of the frozen food industry. And last October he was Thomas Crapper, the guy who invented the modern-day flush toilet.

It killed me remembering that.

"Remember last Halloween? Remember Mick?"

I'm sure Zoe was sort of shocked by the question.

She didn't answer. I mean she *couldn't,* you know? Not without laughing.

"Come on, Zo. You remember."

I don't know why I wanted to hear her say it. I just did.

Finally she made the attempt. "Thomas Cra—"

But even before the Crapper was out of her mouth, she busted out laughing. And then I did too.

Which probably sounds terrible and all. But I promise it wasn't.

The Serengeti Sucks

It was after seven when I finally heard the doorbell ring. I ran into the living room just as my father was coming inside.

"How's Mick? Is he okay, Pop? Is he gonna be all right?"

My father didn't answer. Instead, he put his arms around me and pulled me close. Then he sort of cradled my head in his hand. Real gentle. Like I would break.

It made me scared as anything. I tried to push away to see his face, but he wouldn't let go.

I pushed once more. Only harder this time.

It took him by surprise, I think. And he quick turned his face away from me. But not before I saw him wipe his eyes on his coat sleeve.

I froze with fear.

"Pop?"

He pulled me close again.

Then—in a voice so faint I could barely hear him—he whispered the words "He's gone."

When we walked across the street that night, I held on to my father with both arms. My feet kept tripping over his and twice we almost fell down. But I couldn't let go.

The house was dark when we went inside. The only light was this dim glow coming from underneath my parents' bedroom door. It gave me the chills to see that.

Right away I started turning on the lights. All of them, I mean. Every switch I came to. Even the little bulb over the kitchen stove.

I still hadn't cried. It wasn't that kind of pain yet. Mostly it was just this total feeling of emptiness in my gut. Like a cannonball had been shot cleanly through my middle. And I swear to God, I actually remember reaching under my sweatshirt and touching my stomach to see if you could feel the hole from the outside.

After all the lights were on, I went back to the kitchen, where my father was. And he was just standing there, you know? Right in the center of the room. With his arms hanging limp at his sides.

He sat down for a second, then got right up again. "I should go check on your mother. The doctor gave her some kind of pill to help her sleep."

I nodded. Then I watched him go down the hall. He was walking real slow, like an old man almost. Only when he got across from Mick's room, he stopped altogether, and started running his fingers through his hair. Like you do when you're worried about some big, important decision you have to make.

Then his hand reached out and closed my brother's door.

"NO! DON'T DO THAT! I DON'T WANT YOU TO DO THAT!" I screamed.

Pop pulled his hand away so fast it was like the doorknob had caught on fire.

I ran to where he was standing.

"Please, Pop," I begged. "Please."

I pushed Mick's door open again. "Please."

My father broke down then. Heaving these terrible sobs into his hands. I went numb when I heard that. I couldn't move, couldn't do anything to comfort him. It's just so scary, you know? Hearing your pop cry like that. Even after he had gone into his room, I still couldn't get the sound of it out of my mind.

I think that's when it first hit me that we were in *way* over our heads on this one. This was one of those tragedies that needed a family that knew what it was doing. Like the Kennedys or the Queen of England and her whole bunch.

Not a family like ours that comes unglued if someone doesn't follow the morning bathroom schedule.

I don't know how long I stood there in the

hall that night. All I remember is when I looked up, the lights from the hall were reflecting off Mick's dresser mirror. And I saw the pictures of Wocket stuck all around the frame.

Wocket was our dog. Mick named her. It was before he could pronounce his *r*'s.

She was part basset hound and part beagle. We got her for Christmas when Mick was three. She was supposed to be for both of us. But the day before New Year's, Wocket chewed up my Malibu Barbie and spit out the blond hair in her dog dish. So after that, the two of us weren't all that close.

She really loved Mick, though. She followed him around like a shadow, practically. And when he finally started kindergarten, she'd carry his favorite stuffed animal—this dirty skunk named Stinky—in her mouth all day until he got home.

Wocket was more like a friend to Mick than a pet. He actually discussed things with her, I mean. And instead of teaching her dog tricks, he taught her human stuff, like how to untie his shoelaces and open the bathroom door.

He also taught her to wear a red cowboy hat. Which sounds stupid, I guess. But Wocket really came to love that hat. In the mornings she wouldn't go outside until Mick put it on her head and pulled her ears through these special slits he had cut in the sides.

It's been over a year since we had to have her put to sleep. She had bone cancer, and she was in a lot of pain. So it's not like we had a choice or anything.

We all went to the vet with her that day. But Mick was the only one who went in the room with her when it happened. When he came out, his shirt was covered with Wocket's fur from where he had been hugging her till the very end. He wasn't crying, though. And I remember wondering how in the world he could stay so strong.

The next afternoon after *Gilligan's Island,* the clock in the living room started to chime and Mick automatically got off the couch to go fix Wocket her dinner.

He was halfway to the kitchen before he remembered.

He stopped real sudden in the hall and just

stood there a second. Then he ran into the bathroom and threw up.

My mother knocked on the door, but he told her to go away. As soon as she'd left, he went to his room and didn't come out for hours.

That night, Mick came to the dinner table wearing Wocket's red cowboy hat on his head. It wasn't on purpose, I don't think. He'd been wearing it all afternoon and had just forgotten it was there.

He talked about her the whole time we ate. Telling us his favorite Wocket stories and all. Then after dinner, he took me back to his room and showed me this little pile of her fur he had collected from off the rug and his shirt and other places. He'd put it in a baggie and had it on display on his bookshelf. It was just so touching, you know?

A couple of minutes later, he caught a glimpse of himself in the mirror and realized he was still wearing her hat. His face went totally sad.

"What if I forget her, Phoeb? If I forget her, it'll be like she was never even here."

So that night, me and Mick went through all the family albums, finding pictures of Wocket and sticking them into the sides of his mirror to make sure he'd never forget.

He didn't either. From then on, whenever he went in his room, the first thing he'd do was look at his mirror.

"Hiya, Wocket. How ya doin', girl?" he'd say. "You doin' okay today?"

And I don't think I ever loved my brother more than when I heard him talk to those pictures. I swear to God I don't.

It's weird remembering that now. Because after the accident, I was never once tempted to look through our family album for pictures of Mick. In fact, looking at his picture made me feel sick inside.

We didn't tell our favorite Mick stories at dinner, either. We didn't even eat dinner, really. None of us had an appetite. And besides, no one wanted to sit at the table with his empty chair right in front of our faces. So we mostly just ate cereal standing up if we got hungry. Which was never. So no problem.

Our lives got simpler in other ways, too.

Like we didn't talk that much because nothing seemed important enough to say.

And even though the TV was always on, we almost never sat down to watch it. Every show seemed stupid. Even the news seemed stupid.

Pop and I did try to watch the Discovery Channel one night. But it was all about the Serengeti Plain in Africa, and every scene had some animal being killed by some other animal. We turned it off just as a cheetah was about to pounce on one of those springy little antelope things. I mean who needs to see that, you know?

"The Serengeti sucks," I said.

Usually I don't say "sucks" in front of my father. He thinks it's crude. But this time he nodded and said, "Yeah. It does."

We both went to bed then.

It was eight o'clock.

My mother was already asleep, by the way.

The pills the doctor had given her were still working their magic.

By the third night, her schedule had become pretty predictable. She'd take a pill right about six-thirty. And she'd be out like a light by seven. I wouldn't see her again until ten or eleven the next morning.

She was in her pajamas all the time. She didn't comb her hair. And her face was always puffy from a combination of sleep and crying.

It was pretty depressing. But I couldn't really blame her for wanting to be knocked out. I mean grieving isn't exactly the kind of activity that makes you want to leap out of bed in the morning and get "up and at 'em."

I used to think that when someone dies, the family stays real busy making "arrangements." But for us, it wasn't that way at all.

Since Mick had wanted to be cremated, it was going to be a few days before we'd have his ashes back for interment (another name for burial, I learned). Meanwhile, there was a memorial service to plan. But after only one meeting at the house with our minister, even that had been taken care of.

We did get a lot of phone calls, though. Like I talked to my nana from Florida almost every day, practically. She was planning to stay with us after the memorial service and she was all worried about idiotic stuff like plane arrivals and how long she should stay.

But no matter who called—or for what reason—sooner or later they almost always got around to saying something about God. And how he had a plan for Mick and all. That's when I'd say I had to go and I'd hang up on them. I mean forgive me, okay? But even now I don't feel like giving God a big pat on the back for his wonderful plan.

I answered the doorbell once in a while. It was usually a neighbor with food—which really killed me, 'cause, like I said, we had no appetites. But still, Mrs. Fischer brought potato salad, and Mr. Penski brought a ham-and-potato casserole, and Zoe's mom dropped off potatoes au gratin, and Mrs. Davenport from Pop's work sent over something labeled "Mashed Potato Bake."

Also, a woman I didn't know showed up at the door one night with lime Jell-O in the shape of a heart.

"Does it have potatoes in it?" I asked. She told me to get my father.

I didn't, though. Pop hadn't shaved for days. And his clothes were a wrinkly mess from being slept in. Plus he had on slipper socks. And when anyone in your family is wearing slipper socks, you pretty much have an obligation to keep the outside world from seeing them, I think.

Not that I looked too good myself. I'm not saying that. Mostly I just wore sweats. The same ones I'd been wearing at soccer practice that day, actually. Only now instead of running sprints, my main exercise was walking to the kitchen and pouring cereal I couldn't eat into a bowl, then dumping it down the garbage disposal and walking back to my room again.

The nights were unbelievably long. I never stayed asleep for more than an hour at a time. But I swear to God, I never knew how long the dark could last, until the third night after Mick died. That was the night I cried so hard my stomach muscles hurt when I touched them, and my sheets and pillowcase got so soggy with tears and sweat, I got out of bed and lay on the floor till morning.

I made it through, though. And looking back, I realize I probably even lost a pound or two.

That's the upside of depression, in case you didn't know it. The weight loss, I mean. Nature balances out your grief by letting you slim down. Then at the funeral, people can say you look good in your clothes and really mean it.

Nature's real thoughtful that way.

Treasures

Zoe called me a lot and tried to talk, but I never had much to say. Gossip about school seemed totally stupid. And the really big stuff—about the accident and all—well, it just felt pretty private, that's all.

We did have one conversation, though. She called me after school on Thursday and told me Mrs. Berryhill had brought in this psychologist to talk to Mick's friends about the accident. He was called a *grief* counselor. Which sounds totally depressing. But Zo said he was kind of young, with longish hair, and he had on jeans.

"You wouldn't believe how many kids showed up to meet with him, Phoebe. So many came we had to move out of a regular classroom and into the cafeteria."

I think this is where I was supposed to act real delighted with the turnout or something. I didn't, though. I mean we weren't exactly talking about a bake sale here.

Zoe softened her voice. "All I'm trying to tell you is that you're not alone, Phoebe. A lot of his friends are hurting, too. Like Danny Monroe kept blowing his nose the whole time. And Rickie Bowie had his hat pulled down so far you couldn't see his face."

I rolled my eyes.

"Nobody could even say Mick's name at first," she told me. "That's how bad it was. But then the counselor said that talking about him and saying his name were two of the ways we can sort of keep him with us, you know? And so we did it, Phoebe. All of us. At the same time. We all said 'Mick.' You should have heard it. His name filled up that whole big room, almost. And then we did it again. Only this time it was even louder. And the counselor said—"

I hung up on her. I know it was wrong to do that, but I didn't *care* what the counselor said. And I didn't care about how much better everybody felt after saying his name.

I didn't feel better. I would *never* feel better. Feeling better sounded almost disloyal, if you want to know the truth. And just to make sure I stayed as depressed and loyal as possible, I stopped in Mick's doorway on the way back to my room.

I hadn't stopped there since the night of the accident. It just felt so different now, you know? So private. And off limits. Like a church altar or a cemetery or something.

His door was still open. Pop hadn't tried to shut it again.

I looked in at all the stuff on his shelves, the tons of souvenirs and crap he'd collected over the years. It was mostly junk, but Mick called them his *treasures*. That killed me. His treasures.

Like on the first shelf of his bookcase, he had

the stupidest autograph collection you've ever seen. It was just these two old scraps of paper in a plastic cover. One of them was signed by Herb Fogg, the weatherman on Channel 3. The other was from some guy named Tweets who had been dressed in a bird suit at a local pet store opening.

The second shelf was where he kept his favorite paperbacks—joke books and mysteries mostly. It's also where he kept the ceramic eyeball he'd made in art class one year. The day he brought it home, he snuck it into a package of defrosted chicken that my mother was fixing for dinner. You could hear her scream all over the neighborhood.

"God, that was funny," I said out loud.

Over on his nightstand was the unopened cigar he'd found in the street coming home from kindergarten one day. It was the kind that new fathers hand out when their wives have a baby. The kind that has "IT'S A GIRL!" on the paper band at the top. But at the time, Mick thought it meant the cigar was a girl, and he named it Helen.

There was a flyswatter on his nightstand too. It was part of a set, actually. The other two were hanging from a hook near his closet door.

Mick had a *thing* about flies, I guess you'd call it. It started when he did a science report in second grade and found out that when a fly lands on your sandwich, it vomits on your bread. After that, whenever he saw one he pretty much went berserk until he killed it.

He asked for the set of swatters for Christmas that year. He wanted two for his room (one was a "backup"), and another one that he could take to baseball practice and other outdoor activities during fly season. He called it his mobile field unit (MFU).

The MFU didn't work out that well, though. It was way too long for his back pocket and the swatter part kept rubbing on his shirt, which totally made him sick, 'cause of the fly guts and all. So that's pretty much why he didn't have it with him at the Pricketts' neighborhood Fourth of July barbecue the next year.

It turned out to be a mistake, by the way. All afternoon this huge green fly kept landing

44

on the baked beans. And for two solid hours Mick stood at the food table flailing his arms, screaming, "GET OUT OF HERE! BEGONE!"

Seriously. He said "Begone."

Mr. Morley from down the street asked my mother if he was in therapy.

The memory of that made me grin. And without even thinking about it, I walked into his room and put the swatter on the hook with the others.

"You finally killed that sucker, remember?" I said. "It landed on Mrs. Prickett as she was refilling the potato salad, and you swatted her in the head with your flip-flop."

I laughed out loud. And as soon as I did, my arms were instantly covered in goose bumps.

Because I swear to God, for just a second, I had the most incredible feeling that somewhere Mick was laughing too.

My mother was sitting at the table when I walked into the kitchen that afternoon. She had just gotten out of the shower and was all dressed for bed again.

I sat down in the chair next to her and waved my fingers hello.

We hadn't been talking that much, her and me. Hardly at all, in fact. But I wanted to now. Or *needed* to, I guess you'd say.

"Mom . . . I was sort of wondering . . . do you think he can hear us?"

My mother shut her eyes tight. "Phoebe, please."

"Yeah, I know, but just think about it a second, okay? I mean wouldn't that be so great? If he could hear us when we talk? 'Cause, see, I was in his room just now and . . ."

My mother put her hands over her ears and stood up. Then before I even knew what was happening, she had hurried out the back door and shut it hard behind her.

It had been raining most of the day. But now the rain had turned to mist. And through the glass I watched her walk to the middle of the wet yard and sit down in a lawn chair with her back to me.

For the next few seconds I struggled not to cry.

46

Then all of a sudden, it was like something exploded inside me, and I ran to the door and pulled it open wide.

"THIS ISN'T ONLY ABOUT *YOU*, MOTHER! I LOVED HIM TOO, YOU KNOW! I MISS HIM TOO!"

I slammed the door so hard I thought the glass would break into a million pieces. Then I charged right through the house and straight out the front door.

And it was weird, too, because even though I hadn't thought about where I was going, I automatically headed for school. Running. As fast as I could. To where the accident had happened.

It sounds morbid. I know it does. But all I wanted to do was feel close to my brother. And so in my mind, I wasn't running to the place he had died. I was just running to the last place he had *been*.

Someone had placed a flower there.

I started crying then. Not loud, I don't mean. There were just some tears.

I brushed them away with the back of my hand. And without taking my eyes off the flower, I slowly sat down on the curb.

It was after dark when I finally got up and headed back home.

Tap Dancing on God's Piano

I tend to be very rebellious at times. That's what it says in the comment section on my first-grade report card:

Phoebe tends to be very rebellious at times.

I hated my first-grade teacher, by the way. She tended to be an old bat at times.

Still, I have to admit I can get a little disobedient with authority figures now and then. Okay, I can get a *lot* disobedient. But the way I treated my mother after our little scene in the kitchen was an all-time low for me.

I started saying Mick's name. At every opportunity, I mean.

Not to her face. But if she was in hearing distance, I'd find a way to mention him to anyone I could. Real loud. So she couldn't miss it.

Like the next morning when this delivery boy from the florist knocked on the door with our millionth sympathy bouquet, I started blurting out all this stuff about Mick's favorite flower.

"You probably think it's weird for a boy to have a favorite flower," I said. "But my brother totally loved this one kind called Venus's-flytrap. Ever heard of it? It eats flies. Eats 'em *alive,* I mean. Mick sort of had this thing about flies. An obsession, you might call it."

The boy started backing out of the doorway. I followed him out to the porch.

"They vomit on your bread, you know."

The kid ended up running back to his truck. It was pretty funny, actually. In a gruesome sort of way.

That afternoon, I told our mail carrier about the time Mick put a rubber snake in the mailbox.

"You should have been there," I told her. "The guy screamed the *s* word and threw our mail all over the sidewalk."

Our mail carrier didn't even crack a smile. Instead, she informed me that putting a snake in a mailbox was a federal offense, and she wrote my name down.

"You know, you people take your jobs way too serious," I said.

When I shut the door, my mother was standing there looking at me. There were tears streaming down her face.

"Why are you doing this?" Her voice sounded like a little kid's.

"Doing what? What am I doing?" I tried to be cool as anything. But inside I was filling up with this awful kind of shame I'd never even felt before.

I left her standing there and went straight to my room.

Then I curled up on my bed and my stomach tied itself up in a million knots as I thought about what I had done. There was no getting around it—I had flat-out spent my entire day *taunting* my mother with her dead son's name.

What's next, Phoebe? Want to try imitating his voice or running into her bedroom dressed in his clothes? Boy, that'd really get her, wouldn't it?

I stared hard at the ceiling. *God,* how I hated this. All of it. Myself. My life. My new "family of three."

Mick was dead, and in just a few days we had all turned into people I didn't even know. My mother was a zombie. My father was some slob in slipper socks. And I was a jolly little monster who got my kicks by tormenting Mom with my brother's name.

I clenched my fist.

"*Damn* you, Mick. *Damn* you for doing this to us," I whispered, and then the tears started streaming down my face, too.

I was still crying when I finally reached for the phone and called Zo.

"Oh Jesus, Zoe, what's happening to me?

52

I swear to God, I just don't know what's happening."

On the other end of the line you could practically hear Zo rolling up her sleeves to get right to work.

We started talking then. Really talking for the first time since Mick had died. Talking about my parents. And the accident. And how horrible and confused I felt inside.

And missing Mick, of course. The conversation always came back to missing Mick. And loving him. And worrying about him.

Mostly Zo just listened. Even when I started saying the same stuff over and over again, she acted like she was hearing it for the first time.

I could always talk to her after that too. Always. No matter what I was feeling.

The interment of Mick's ashes was at four-thirty that same afternoon. We were home by five.

At midnight, I got out of bed and dialed Zoe's number again.

I knew it would wake up her parents, but I didn't much care. After you've been to your brother's interment, waking people in the middle of the night doesn't bother you a bit.

Zo picked up on the first ring. "H'lo?"

I didn't say anything. She knew it was me, though. Me and Zoe sort of have a psychic thing going, sometimes.

"Phoebe?"

I nodded.

"You okay?" she asked.

I took a shaky breath.

"No."

She came right over.

We got blankets from my bedroom and covered up on the living room couch so my parents wouldn't hear us. But even before we were settled in, I had already started to tell her about it.

"It only took about ten minutes," I said. "It was just a few prayers at the grave. And there were only four of us there. Just my parents and me and the minister . . .

"And, well, you know. The urn was there too. It was box-shaped. Except it was made out of marble or granite or something. Small, though. Like about the size of a shoe box, I'd say. Which is why it wasn't as sad as a regular funeral, I think. 'Cause it was almost like he wasn't even there, you know? Like there wasn't a trace of him left, hardly.

"Only see, that's what's starting to get to me. I mean where *is* he, Zoe? Right now. Right at this very minute."

She looked a little confused. "He's in *heaven,* Phoeb. We talked about all that this afternoon, remember?"

"Yeah, but what does that even *mean* . . . heaven? Because see, I need to be able to *put* him somewhere, Zo. In my head, I mean. I need to be able to close my eyes and picture him and know he's okay. And just saying the word *heaven* doesn't help that much. Because like what is heaven, exactly? And where is it? And what do you do there?"

Zoe shrugged. "I don't know. I guess I always just figured it was up. Like in the clouds or something."

I stared at her curiously. "That's what you actually *think,* Zo? You actually think that after you die, you float up to the clouds? And do what? Sprout a halo and play the harp?"

She frowned. "Don't make fun of me, Phoebe. It's just that I've never thought much about heaven's specific location, okay? And anyway, the important thing is that heaven is where God is."

I rolled my eyes. "Yes, but that still doesn't *tell* me anything, Zoe. I mean what does it look like there? And what in the world do you do all day?"

Things didn't get better. Zoe said, "You do God stuff."

My mouth practically dropped open with that one. "*God stuff*? What the heck is God stuff? You mean like right now you think Mick is reading Bible stories, and going around saying 'Peace be with you,' and junk? Because that's a little hard to believe, don't you think? Especially considering he got suspended from choir practice last year for tap dancing on the piano."

Zoe flopped back on her pillow. "Hey, I've got an idea. Why don't you just tell me what you want me to say, and I'll say it. That way, you won't have to keep mocking me. . . ."

We didn't talk for a while after that.

"I'm sorry, okay?" I said finally. "I didn't mean to make fun of you. It's just that everyone seems to have all these easy answers. Only none of them make any sense to me.

"Like my nana from Florida keeps saying this is all part of God's plan for Mick. And we're not allowed to question the plan, or think that maybe the plan stinks. We just have to accept it. Period. The end.

"And my other grandmother says that God must have needed Mick more than we did. Only what kind of a selfish God is that? To just snatch somebody away from the people who love him? Not to mention the fact that it's a little hard to believe that the most powerful being in the entire universe needs a seventh-grader who can't even program a VCR without screwing up the TV."

Zoe frowned in thought. "So maybe your grandmothers are wrong," she said. "Maybe Mick's accident wasn't planned at all. Maybe it was a real, honest-to-goodness accident, and God is just as sad about it as everybody else."

I nodded. "Yeah. Well, that's sort of what I've been thinking too. Only that would mean that God had no control over it. And if God has no control, then he can't be all that powerful, can he? Unless, of course, he makes it a rule not to interfere in our lives or something. Or who knows? Maybe there isn't a God at all. Only I don't even want to *consider* that option right now.

"The point is, there's no way to know any of this stuff for absolute, positive sure. Just like there's no way to know what Mick's doing right now. Or who he's with. Or if he's lonely. Or scared."

I stopped for a second. "You don't think he's scared, do you, Zo? 'Cause I hate it when I think about that. But the idea keeps coming into my head. And I can't get it to stay away."

Just then my throat began to ache the way it does when you're trying not to cry. "Or maybe he's not even out there at all. I mean maybe he's just gone, period."

I swallowed hard. "Oh God, Zo. I want so bad to know he's okay. But I keep trying to picture him in my head. And I can't. 'Cause I just don't know where to put him anymore."

Zoe reached out her arms to me. And when she did, I caved in. Totally, I mean. Sobbing out of control.

She rubbed my back and waited for the worst of it to be over. And then, out of thin air, these magical words came out of her mouth.

"Put him everywhere, why don't you?"

It stunned me when she said that. I don't know why, exactly. But when I looked at Zoe's face, I could tell that she was almost as surprised as I was.

She shrugged. "It just sort of came to me," she said. "But it makes sense, don't you think, Phoeb? Because like if God is everywhere the way they say he is, and Mick is with God, then Mick could be everywhere too."

She raised her eyebrows. "Couldn't he?"

For a second I couldn't even answer. I was still just so amazed, you know? At how *right* it felt.

"Then he could *hear* me, Zoe," I whispered. My stomach filled with butterflies.

Slowly, I leaned back on the couch and tried to let it all sink in.

At the other end, Zo pulled the blankets up around her chin. And for a long time neither of us said a word.

I thought she had fallen asleep, when I felt her tap me on the foot.

"Phoeb?"

"Yeah?"

"I could be wrong, you know. He could just be up in the clouds tap dancing on God's piano."

I hit her with my pillow.

Getting a Grip

The memorial service was on Saturday. Like I said, there was never any doubt that Mick had wanted to be cremated. He'd made up his mind about it last year when my Great-grandmother Harte died.

He and I weren't really that close to our great-grandmother. She'd been in a nursing home for most of our lives, and she was over ninety when she died. So I can't say that I grieved that much. Or at all, actually.

Mick was more upset than I was. As soon as

she was gone, he started feeling guilty that he hadn't spent more time with her.

"I should have gotten you to take me out there more often," he told Pop. "I could have taught her how to play Pictionary or something."

But even though Mick felt bad that she had died, the thought of going to her funeral gave him the creeps. The morning of the service, he told my father that Great-grandmother had appeared to him in the bathroom mirror and told him she didn't want him to come.

Pop put his hands on Mick's shoulders and said a bunch of stuff about "looking life's difficult moments squarely in the face and coming out a better man."

Then he gave Mick a hearty squeeze and said, "In other words . . . go put on your suit."

The funeral was at the chapel in the nursing home. The casket was open. So you could see the body. That's what they call you after you die, by the way. They call you "the body."

When Mick first saw it from the hall, he actually gasped.

"Oh God, she's . . . she's *there*!" he said.

The next thing I knew, he was squatting down by the entrance, taking these real deep breaths like he had just run a marathon or something.

"Ho boy, ho boy," he said. He was sweating like a pig.

Pop tried to pick him up. But Mick stayed frozen in his squatting position, so my father was forced to set him back down.

"Don't make me go in there, Pop," he begged. "I mean I realize a lot of people are okay with this sort of thing. But I think it's pretty clear that I'm not handling this with the dignity we had both hoped for."

My father told him to get a grip. "The only way to conquer your fears is to face them head-on," he said.

Then he picked Mick up again and shook him a little bit till his legs unfolded. After that, he took him by the hand and led him inside.

Big mistake.

By then Mick had worked himself into such a state of panic that when he saw the body up close in her curly wig and red hat, he became sort of mesmerized, you know? He couldn't take his eyes off her. But it wasn't until he spotted the lace hankie in her hand that the pressure really got to him.

I felt him tap me on the shoulder.

"Do you think she'll be blowing her nose anytime soon?" he blurted.

Then he busted out in this wild hysterical laughter that I knew he had no hope of controlling.

My father snapped his fingers at him. So loud you wouldn't believe. And since Mick couldn't quit laughing, Pop just kept snapping and snapping, until it sounded like he was keeping time to the funeral music that was being piped in over the loudspeaker.

Finally, my mother grabbed my father's hand to stop him and told Mick to please wait outside until the ceremony was over.

On the way home, my father started a lecture on humiliating your family in public.

Mom told him to knock it off. "This isn't Mick's fault, Ed. He told you he couldn't handle it and you insisted on dragging him in there anyway." Then she rolled her eyes and added,

"And ye gods . . . that *snapping*."

It's kind of satisfying to hear your own father get yelled at. But Mick didn't gloat or anything. Instead, he made the announcement that when he died, he wanted to be recycled into a neat little pile of ashes and buried in a pleasant cemetery somewhere. It sounded pretty nice the way he put it and all.

Mom said for her funeral she wanted a big street parade like they have in New Orleans— with a Dixieland jazz band playing and people strutting all over the place with umbrellas.

Pop promised that's exactly what he would do if she died first. Then as soon as her back was turned, he made the cuckoo sign at her.

Getting dressed for Mick's memorial service was awful. I mean if ever there's a time when you shouldn't be caring what you look like, your brother's funeral is pretty much it. But still, in the back of your head, you just keep thinking about all those people who are going to be looking at you. People you haven't seen for years, probably. And the next thing you know, you're weaving a black velvet ribbon into your hair. And trying to track down the right purse to go with your shoes.

My parents and I drove to the church in total silence. I sat in the back, careful not to cross the imaginary line that had always divided the seat into "Mick's side" and "my side."

Mom was sitting right in front of me. I stared at the back of her head and wondered why I'd never noticed the strands of gray that were mixed in with her dark brown hair.

Then suddenly it dawned on me that the reason I hadn't seen them before was because they'd never *been* there before. And it made me feel so sick with sympathy I reached out and touched her hair.

As soon as my mother felt my fingers, she put her hand over mine. Then with her other hand, she reached for Pop. And that's how we rode the rest of the way to church. Connected like a family chain, sort of. With one link missing.

It was crowded when we got there. But the front pew had been reserved for us. We were celebrities. And when we walked in the church, still holding hands, the whole place got totally quiet.

I kept telling myself, "Act natural, act natural." But the entire time I was saying it in my head, it just struck me as wrong, you know? That at a time like this, I should have to work so hard to please others with my behavior.

When the service finally started, I tried to concentrate on my prayers. And after that, the stories.

That's mostly what the service was—stories about him. Our minister had suggested that people bring their favorite memories about Mick to the church. And whoever wanted to could go to the microphone and share them.

The school janitor went first. His name is Mr. Finnius. He and Mick had been friends since kindergarten, I think it was. He told about the time Mick got his head caught in the wrought-iron railing in front of the main office and Mr. Finnius got him out by smearing Crisco in his hair.

People laughed, which sounded weird because you almost never hear people cracking up in church. It's kind of too bad, when you think about it. I mean I bet you anything God would rather hear laughing than all that crying and begging for forgiveness people dump on him every week.

Mick's kindergarten teacher went to the microphone next. She told about the spring pageant, when Mick broke away from the Dance of the Bumblebees and started spinning wildly all over the stage, doing a dance completely his own. After the show—when she asked him why he'd done it—he told her that "the music got in his pants."

There were lots of other stories, too. Each one of them seemed funnier than the one before it. And when the last person sat down, I swear it was like the whole mood in the church had changed. There was just this kind of joy that I can't even explain. And I mean it was so *like* Mick, you know? To be able to make people laugh at his own service that way.

I went last. I didn't want to go at all. But it seemed sort of right that somebody from our family should say a few words. And since neither of my parents thought they could handle it, I had told them I'd try.

When I walked to the microphone, my heart was pounding so hard in my chest I was sure I'd have some sort of attack before I got there. But once I'd made it to the front, I took a couple of deep breaths and got on with it.

"My mom wanted me to read you her favorite Mother's Day card from Mick," I said. I held it up for them to see.

Then I told them about how Mick had been in fifth grade when he wrote it. And how he and my mother had been arguing all week about this one certain thing that Mick really wanted but that Mom positively refused to let him have.

"On the Friday morning before Mother's Day, they'd had another battle," I said. "And Mick left the house totally annoyed with her. Except, as it turned out, that was the day they were making these cards in art."

I smiled a little. "Mick told the teacher that he wasn't in the right mood to make a card for his mom. Then the teacher told Mick to get in the mood or get an F."

I held up the card and showed it again. Slower this time. So everyone could see the sloppy wad of lace glued to the paper. And the word "MA" scribbled in pencil at the top.

I opened the card and read it out loud.

"Roses are red,
Violets are blue.
I still don't know why
I can't get a tattoo.

Your son,
Mick Harte"

Dogs Can Laugh in Heaven

I went back to school the Tuesday after the memorial service.

That's when I found out I was famous.

Zoe and I were walking into the building, when we passed a bunch of sixth-graders standing outside the door. As I reached for the door handle, I heard one of them say, "Hey, look. There's the sister of the dead kid."

My blood went cold when I heard that. And my stomach heaved so violently I thought I might get sick.

I ran inside and ducked into the girls' bathroom. But by the time I got there, the shock had worn off and I was just plain mad.

"Ignore him," said Zoe. "The kid's a total moron."

But she knew there was no way I could ignore something like that. And a second later, I was outside again, pushing my way through the crowd of kids till I found the creep who'd said it.

I shoved him up against the wall and pointed my finger in his face.

"Don't you *ever* call my brother 'the dead kid' again, do you hear me? His name was Mick Harte. And from now on, if you want to talk about him—which you're not even fit to do—you use his name. You got that, creep? Do you *have* that?"

When Zoe pulled me away, I was shaking so hard I couldn't stop. I didn't care, though. It was right for me to do that. And I'd do it again. I swear to God I would.

I wasn't sure what to expect when I went to my first class. In the back of my mind, I suppose I thought it would be a little like the memorial service. People would come up and say they were sorry and all. Then I'd say thanks or something equally stupid. But we'd get through it.

Only as it turned out, it was a lot easier than I imagined. Because nothing happened at all. That is, unless you count how quiet the room got when I walked in. And how everyone pretended they weren't really looking at me, when the whole time they were plainly sneaking peeks as I walked to my desk.

All except Eileen Fentendorf, that is. Eileen turned right around in her chair and followed me straight to my seat.

I stared at her until she turned back. Don't ever get into a staring contest with me, by the way. You'll never win.

Eileen Fentendorf knows that now. She was in three of my morning classes and I stared her down in every one of them.

Just for the record, though, by lunchtime not one single person had come up to me to say they were sorry.

No one had even said Mick's name.

"They're not trying to be mean, Phoebe. They just don't know what to say," Zoe told me.

I tried to shrug it off. "Yeah, well, no big deal," I said.

But when we sat down to eat and my so-called *real* friends waved from the other end of the lunch table and quick looked away, I finally lost it.

I glared at them like you wouldn't believe. "I'm not going to go nuts if you talk about him, you know. What's wrong with you guys, anyway? Didn't you go to grief counseling? Zoe said you were there. But you must not have been listening. 'Cause we're all supposed to be saying Mick's name, remember?"

Cara Cook looked totally mortified. "Yeah, but we just weren't sure if we should or not, Phoebe. I mean we didn't want to make you feel worse or anything."

Yeah, right. Like that was even possible.

Then all at once, Lindy Nelson sort of lunged for my hand, and squeezed it way too tight. And Amy Lightner blurted out something incredibly stupid, about how her mother said to say hi to my mother.

I pretty much learned my lesson after that. I didn't force them to talk anymore. Mostly I just sat there staring at my hoagie while the three of them crammed their lunches down their throats so they could get the heck away from me. Their mouths were still full when they took their trays back.

After they were gone, I put my head down on the table, and I didn't move. Not even after the bell rang.

Zoe stayed with me till the cafeteria had emptied. Then I heard her calm, quiet voice next to my ear. "Phoebe, I think you should go to the nurse and ask her to let you go home."

I nodded blankly and stood up. Zo walked me to the hall. I never made it all the way to the nurse, though. To get to her office, you have to go through the main reception area, and Mrs. Berryhill was there. As soon as she saw me, she put her arm around me and steered me through her door.

It's too bad she didn't have a clue about the kind of mood I was in. Maybe then she wouldn't have been so quick to tell me about how she had *lost* her own mother two years ago, and how *losing* a family member is the worst kind of pain there is, and how in time I would learn to accept my *loss* and go on.

I stood up.

"He's not my *loss,* Mrs. Berryhill," I told her. "I didn't just misplace him or leave him behind on a bus somewhere. He died, okay? Mick died. But he will never—ever—be *lost*. So, please. Do not say that word to me one more time."

I didn't wait for her to reply. I just turned around and ran out of her office as fast as I could. I didn't stop, either. I kept right on going—out of the building, down the block, and up the street to my house.

Nana from Florida was already talking to Mrs. Berryhill on the phone. I ignored her fingers snapping at me as I blitzed down the hall to Mick's room. Then quietly, I pulled his door shut behind me.

This time, I had known from the start where

I was headed. I went straight to Mick's bed and crawled underneath his covers.

Then I buried my face in his pillow.

And I breathed in the smell of him.

In my dream, I was sitting in Mrs. Berryhill's office—only her office wasn't inside the school. It was outside—in the middle of a forest—which I realize sounds totally stupid. But in dreams, stuff like that seems perfectly normal.

Anyway, at first Mrs. Berryhill was nowhere in sight. But then I looked into the woods and saw her darting in and out from behind the trees, the way cartoon characters do sometimes when they're trying to find someone.

"HEY, MRS. BERRYHILL, WHO'RE YOU LOOKIN' FOR?" I shouted out. Only she was too far away to hear me.

That's when I decided to help her in her search, and I stood up on her chair and hollered out, "OLLI-OLLI-OXIN-FREE!" Which is sort of this international kids' language for "Come out, come out, wherever you are." And so I wasn't surprised when I heard a bunch of feet running through the forest in my direction.

Only the weird thing was, the feet didn't belong to a kid. They belonged to *Wocket*. Our old dog. She trotted out of the trees, happy as anything, wearing her old red cowboy hat, plus these four little red cowboy boots on her feet, which were like the cutest things you've ever seen.

Then right behind her came Mick. He was carrying a box of cereal and wearing this amazing T-shirt that flashed his name on and off in hot-pink neon letters, so like you couldn't forget it even if you tried. M-I-C-K! M-I-C-K! M-I-C-K!

I'm talking about the coolest T-shirt you can imagine. And since he was holding so tight to the cereal box, I figured that's where it must have come from. So, naturally, I tried to grab it to see if there was one in there for me, too. Only—what do you know—Mick refused to hand it over.

The next thing I knew, we were wrestling on top of Mrs. Berryhill's desk. And Mick had me in a sleeper hold, which he thought was pretty funny, I guess, because he was grinning from ear to ear. And Wocket must have thought so too. Because all of a sudden I heard this weird snorting sound. And when I looked on the ground, Wocket was laughing so hard she was rolling on her back with her little boots up in the air.

It was the funniest thing I'd ever seen. So funny I woke myself up laughing. Which I'd never even heard of anyone doing before.

And it must have been loud. Because right away, I heard Mick's door open. I was sure it was Nana from Florida. Coming to yell at me for ditching school.

But it wasn't her at all.

It was my mother. Just standing there, staring at me with this horrible look on her face. And all I could think about was how awful it must be for her. To open the door and see me in Mick's bed like that.

I started to ramble.

"I . . . I had a dream about him."

My mother's eyes closed.

"No, wait, Mom. You don't understand. It was a good dream. It was a funny dream. Wocket was in it too. And so was Mrs. Berryhill. I think that's because when I saw her today, she kept calling Mick my *loss*. But see, he's never going to be lost, Mom. I swear to God he's not. Because Zoe and I sort of figured out that he's everywhere now. And if you're everywhere, then how can you be lost?"

Mom's face softened a little.

"In my dream we were fighting and wrestling around and stuff. But it's okay to remember that we used to fight, don't you think? I mean Mick would probably hate it if we tried to turn him into some perfect little angel or something. 'Cause after all he *did* put a lot of effort into annoying us sometimes, you know."

I stopped for a second. "Like remember how mad we'd all get when he'd do that disgusting fake sneeze on the last piece of pie so nobody else could have it?

"And remember how irritating he was on vacation last summer? You even made him sit in the car when we went to McDonald's that one time. Remember? You said he was demented."

My mother looked away. "Stop it, Phoebe. You know perfectly well I was kidding when I said that."

I tried not to grin. "You were not, Mother. You were furious at him. And you know why, too."

She waited a minute before she spoke again.

"I wasn't furious. I was just irritated. I mean for heaven's sakes, who wouldn't be? He wouldn't stop talking like Elmer Fudd. He talked like Elmer Fudd for three solid days in a row."

I covered my smile with my hand. "You brought him back an Egg McMuffin, remember? And you said if he talked like Elmer Fudd one more time, you weren't going to take him to Disneyland."

I bit my lip. "Remember what he called you then?"

By this time I could tell that my mother was fighting to keep a straight face. She sucked in her cheeks.

"He called me a Wascally Wabbit," she managed.

But as soon as she said it she started to laugh. We both did.

She came into the room then. It must have been unbelievably hard for her to do that. But she came in, and sat down on the edge of his bed.

I made a place for her next to me on Mick's pillow. But for the longest time Mom just sat there. Stroking her fingers lightly over his bedspread.

Then at last she lay down beside me and gently brushed the hair from my eyes. "Tell me some more about your dream," she whispered.

I told her that dogs can laugh in heaven.

That night Nana from Florida made spaghetti for dinner. When I heard her carrying the plates in to set the table, I rushed in there as fast as I could.

"We don't eat in the dining room anymore, Nana. We eat on trays in front of the TV. Remember?"

She waved me away. "Can't eat spaghetti off a tray. Slop it all down the front of you."

"Yeah, I know, Nana. But still, I don't think we should—"

My grandmother's arms flew into the air. "Shoo! Skedaddle! Scat!" she said.

Nana from Florida has cats. It explains a lot.

An hour later, she called us to dinner by banging on the spaghetti pot with a metal spoon. Only when we got there, all the place mats were at the wrong spots. Like my father's place mat was at Mick's old spot, and my mother's iced tea glass was where Pop had always sat. Meanwhile, my milk was right across from him where Mom used to sit. And Nana from Florida was next to me.

Mom was already shaking her head no when my grandmother came through the door with this heavy platter of spaghetti in her hands, hollering, "Hot, hot, hot!"

She hurried to set it down. That's when she noticed us standing there staring at the place mats.

"Oh poop," she said. "I guess crazy old Nana got everyone all catawampus, didn't I?"

Then, as usual, her patience was gone and her hands were waving all around in the air again with that same metal spoon.

"Well, won't kill ya, will it? Sit down before this stuff gets cold."

I was halfway through my spaghetti before I realized what an amazing thing my grandmother had done.

Accidentally on purpose, she had gotten us back to the table. Eating as a family again.

And no one was staring at Mick's empty chair.

Nana from Florida.

Who would have thought it?

Common Sense and Good Judgment

Three blocks from my house, there used to be a dangerous intersection. It was one of those intersections where it was impossible for cars to pull out onto the main street without horns honking and brakes screeching and stuff.

My father griped about it every time we drove through there.

"The city's not going to put a light in here until someone gets hurt," he'd say. "You wait and see. It's going to take an accident before anything gets done."

Last year there were four accidents in seven months and they finally installed a traffic signal.

The first time we drove through it, some guy ran a red light and Pop had to swerve out of the way to keep from hitting him.

It scared us both to death. Pop swore at the guy and then started right in on this lecture about "how you can lead a horse to water, but you can't make him drink."

"It's a sad lesson, Phoebe," he said. "But no matter how many traffic lights they put in, they'll never be able to make people use common sense and good judgment."

As he was talking, he turned around to make sure I was paying attention. While his head was turned, our car drifted into the next lane and two cars blasted their horns at us.

He made a quick recovery. It was close, though.

It was also the end of his talk on good judgment and common sense. And the lesson I ended up learning that day was that even smart guys with chemistry degrees do stupid stuff once in a while.

It's just that usually when you do stupid

stuff, you luck out and get away with it. And if you luck out enough times, it's pretty easy to start believing that you're always going to luck out. *Forever,* I mean.

Like I can't even count how many soccer games I played in without shin guards before I finally got kicked in the leg and started wearing them. Over thirty, though, I bet.

And my mother had never had a major sunburn her whole entire life till she and Pop went to the beach for their anniversary last year. You can still see the blotchy places where her skin peeled from all the blisters, by the way.

And then there was Mick. Who went twelve years and five months without ever falling off his bike.

So he refused to wear a helmet.

And it's the one thing about him that I've tried to forget. And to forgive him for.

And I'm sorry, but I can't seem to do either one.

It was over a week before Mrs. Berryhill called me down to her office again. I was kind of nervous when I got her note. Even though I knew my parents had explained to her about me ditching school that day, part of me was still expecting detention.

That's why I was relieved to see another woman sitting in her office when I walked in. Mrs. Berryhill introduced us. Her name was Mrs. Somebody-or-other from the PTA.

She shook my hand and said how "sincerely sorry" she was about what happened to my brother. Then she started right in on how the PTA wanted to make sure that nothing like that ever happened again, so they were going to sponsor this big assembly on bike safety. It was already in the works, she said. There were going to be police officers, and instructional videos, and demonstrations of the latest safety gear, and yadda, yadda, yadda . . .

"We'd like to invite you to sit onstage with the other speakers," she told me. Then she took my hand again and asked if I thought maybe I could say a few words to my classmates about bike safety. Because a few words from me would have "a tremendous impact," she thought.

And through all of this, I just sort of sat there, you know? Staring at her in disbelief. Because I swear I could not figure out what planet this woman had come from.

I mean where in the world had she ever gotten the nerve to ask me something like that? Had it never even dawned on her that the timing of a bicycle-safety assembly was just a little off for me? That maybe I would have liked to see a safety assembly *before* my brother was killed?

I didn't make a scene. I just stood up and took my hand away.

"I can't," I said.

When I turned to go, Mrs. Somebody-or-other fell all over herself telling me how much she understood.

Which really killed me, by the way.

Because the woman didn't have a clue.

I don't know when I changed my mind about speaking at the assembly.

I think it was just one of those flip-flops you do sometimes. You know, like at first you have this gut reaction to something and you're positive that you're totally right. Only after a while, it creeps into your mind that the other guy may actually have a point. Then the next thing you know, his point's making more sense than your point. Which is totally annoying. But still, it happens.

It used to happen with me and Mick all the time. Like a couple of months ago, we were arguing about whether the Three Stooges were funny or not. I kept saying they were hilarious, and Mick kept saying they were just morons.

Then we started kind of wrestling around a little bit, and the next thing I know, Mick jumps up and starts slapping the top of his head with his hand and fluttering it up and down in front of my face. After that, he grabs my nose with his fist, twists it hard, and finally slaps it away with his other hand. He ended his performance with the classic Three Stooges laugh—Nyuk, nyuk, nyuk—and a quick move to boink my eyes out with his fingers. Fortunately, I was able to block it with my hand.

Mick stopped the routine as fast as he had

started it. Then, without saying a word, he stood up real dignified-like and dusted himself off.

He looked at me without the trace of a smile. "Hilarious, wasn't I?" he said dryly.

"Yes," I lied. "You were."

But deep down I had already started to feel different about the Stooges.

There were eight hundred people in the gym when I walked to the microphone that morning. I wasn't nervous, though, which really surprised me. But I swear I felt almost relaxed when I set down my bag of stuff next to the podium.

"I'm Mick Harte's sister," I said. Then I bent down and reached into my plastic bag.

"When Mick was in third grade, this is what my grandmother from Florida sent him for Christmas."

I held it up. "It's a glow-in-the-dark bow tie with pink flamingos on it."

A couple of kids chuckled a little.

"Don't worry," I said. "He never wore it. He said it made him look like a dork."

There was more laughing then. And I reached into my bag again.

"When Mick was in fourth grade, my Aunt Marge sent him this from Michigan."

I held up a hat in the shape of a trout.

"Mick said this one went beyond dork, all the way to doofus," I said.

This time everybody really cracked up. Some of the kids in the first row even stood up and started craning their necks to see what I would pull out next.

They watched as I turned the bag upside down and a cardboard box fell onto the stage.

Carefully, I set it on the podium and waited for everything to get totally quiet.

"When Mick turned ten, my parents gave him this for his birthday."

I took my time opening the lid. I mean you could really feel the anticipation and all.

But when I finally pulled Mick's gift out of the box—still brand-new—there was just this gasp.

And no one laughed at all.

No one even moved.

"This was my brother's bike helmet," I said.

My voice broke, but somehow I forced myself to finish.

"He said it made him look like a dork."

Forever

don't know if what I said at that assembly will make a difference. I don't know if it will help anyone use better judgment than my brother did. I hope so, though. Honest to God, I do. Because Mick died from a massive head injury. And yet the doctors said that just an inch of Styrofoam would have made the difference between his living and dying.

It's been a month since the accident now. Things have gotten a little better at home. Nana from Florida went back to Orlando. And my mother gets dressed in the mornings, usually.

She's gone back to work, too—just two days a week, but it's a start.

We sit down to dinner every night at our new places. Eating still isn't a big deal with us, though. Like last night we had grilled cheese sandwiches and mashed potatoes. And on Sunday all the forks were in the dishwasher so we ate potato salad with soup spoons. My mother's eased up on stuff like that. Death sort of gives you a new outlook on the importance of proper silverware.

It's called *perspective*. It means your father doesn't iron a crease in his pants every morning. And the hamburgers come in all shapes and sizes.

I've started to laugh more often. But I still feel guilty when I'm having too good a time. Which is totally ridiculous. Because if I want to feel guilty, there're lots better reasons than that. Like I'm just now starting to deal with how Mick asked me to ride his bike home that day and all.

I kept that whole memory tucked away in the back of my mind after the accident happened. But bad memories must grow in the dark, I think, because it kept on creeping into my thoughts, till it was with me almost all the time, it seemed.

Then last Saturday, when my father and I were riding home from a soccer game, my stomach started churning like it always does right before I'm about to blurt out an unplanned confession.

It's one of the sickest feelings there is, by the way. To realize you're about to squeal on yourself like that.

The only thing sicker is keeping it inside.

So it all came busting out. All about how Mick asked me to ride his bike that day. And how I had soccer practice so I told him I couldn't do it.

"See, Pop? Don't you get it? I could have kept the accident from ever happening. If only I had ridden his bike home, Mick would still be here right now."

I was crying a little bit now. But except for handing me the travel tissues from the dashboard, my father hardly seemed to notice.

Instead, he just kept staring out the window at the road in front of us.

Then slowly, he began shaking his head from side to side.

"I'm sorry, Pop. I'm sorry. I'm sorry," I said over and over again.

My face was buried in my hands when I finally felt him touch my shoulder.

"I'm going to make a list, Phoebe," he said. "And I want you to keep a count." His voice was real low and steady as he began.

"*If only* you had ridden Mick's bike home, Mick would still be here.

"*If only* the truck had been going a little faster or a little slower, Mick would still be here.

"*If only* his meeting had been scheduled one day earlier or one day later, Mick would still be here.

"*If only* it had been raining that day, I'd have driven him to school and Mick would still be here.

"*If only* one of his friends had kept him talking a second longer at his locker that afternoon . . .

"*If only* the house he was riding to had been in the other direction . . .

"*If only* that rock hadn't been on the sidewalk at the exact spot . . ."

He stopped then. And I was pretty sure he was finished. But all at once, he heaved this God-awful sigh and whispered, "If only I had made him wear his helmet."

My heart broke for my father at that moment and I reached my hand out to him.

He held on to it tight. Then he smiled the saddest smile you've ever seen.

"What number are we on, little girl?" He sounded so old.

I scooted closer to him.

"I think we're done, Pop," I said softly.

He pressed my hand to his cheek.

The two of us drove home in silence.

Yesterday was the official one-month anniversary of the accident. I used to think that anniversaries only celebrated happy things. But now I know that they're just a way of measuring time.

I went to soccer practice after school. I didn't feel much like running, though. Coach Brodie must have sensed something was wrong, because she didn't push me or yell at me for dogging it, like she usually does.

The weird thing is, after practice was over, I didn't want to leave the field. All I wanted to do was sit on the sidelines by myself for a while. And think about Mick.

It sounds depressing, but it wasn't. I mean there were lots of good memories of Mick at that field too. Living so close to school, we used to go down there all the time and kick the soccer ball around or throw the Frisbee or something.

A couple of months ago, we even tried playing polo on our bikes using my father's golf clubs. It wasn't that much fun, though. I kept hitting myself in the foot with the sand wedge and Mick kept getting the putter caught in his pants.

I grinned at the memory and sat down in the grass.

Unfortunately, right across the field from me, a group of noisy workmen were banging around putting up a new set of permanent bleachers. They were setting them in concrete. So it was pretty clear they were going to be working there for a while.

Even so, I decided to wait them out. It's another talent of mine, I guess you'd say. In addition to staring you down, I can also wait you out.

It was almost dark when they finally went home. I still can't believe no one stayed behind to guard the new sidewalk they'd just poured. I mean you've gotta be nuts leaving wet cement unguarded at a junior high school.

Especially if there's an eighth-grade girl sitting across the field who's been watching you all afternoon. And she's already spotted a little stick lying in the grass next to her hand. Which was totally weird, by the way. Because there's not a tree anywhere near the soccer field. None even in *sight,* I mean. And yet there was this stick.

It can give you the shivers if you think about it too much.

The stick was just the perfect size, too. Small enough to do a neat job, but still strong enough to carve the letters deep into the concrete so they would be there forever.

That's what's so great about cement, you know. The forever part, I mean.

I was totally calm when I did it. I just walked over, bent down, and printed the letters, large and neat and clear as they could be.

M-I-C-K H-A-R-T-E W-A-S H-E-R-E.

I stood up and looked at it.

I smiled.

Mick Harte was here.

And now he's gone.

But for twelve years and five months, my brother was one of the neatest kids you'd ever want to meet.

And I just wanted to tell you about him, that's all.

I just thought you ought to know.

Dear Readers,

Although Mick Harte is a fictional character, the following statistics are all too real:

1) Bicycle accidents are one of the leading causes of accidental deaths of children between 5 and 14.

2) Head injuries are the main cause of death in bicycle crashes.

3) A fall from as little as two feet (2 feet!) can cause *permanent* brain damage.

4) The proper bicycle helmet can reduce head injuries 85% and brain injuries by up to 88%.

Please, don't make Mick Harte's story *your* story.

Wear a helmet when you ride a bike!

Sincerely,

Barbara Park

Can Howard **HANDLE** a new school with **NO** friends?

TURN THE PAGE FOR A PEEK AT

#1 *New York Times* bestselling author of Junie B. Jones

Barbara Park

THE KID IN THE Red Jacket

"Hilarious. Barbara Park makes reading fun."
—Dav Pilkey, author of Captain Underpants

Over half a MILLION sold!

"My leg's hot," I announced as our car pulled out of our driveway.

It was the day of the "big move." At least that's what my parents kept calling it. I hated that. It's not that I didn't realize moving from Arizona to Massachusetts was "big." It's just that when they said it, they made it seem real exciting and fun. They never made it sound like what it really was—rotten.

My mother turned around and gave me one of her looks. "Please, Howard, don't start. We haven't even made it to the street yet."

I glanced over at my baby brother, Gaylord. He was sitting happily in his car seat, staring at his hands. He had just discovered his hands, and he kept opening and closing them like they were some great new invention.

I reached out and touched his leg.

"Gaylord's leg isn't hot," I reported. "Gaylord's in the shade. Has anyone ever noticed how Gaylord always gets the shade? I mean, I'm aware that he's a baby and everything, but I don't think you should play favorites like this. I think we should flip a coin for the shady side."

When no one said anything, I leaned toward him. "What's that, Gaylord?" I asked. "You want what?"

I tapped my father on the shoulder. "Gaylord says he wants to switch places. He says he wants to get some sun on those lily-white legs of his."

My mother just sighed. She probably would have yelled, but I had been making her yell so much lately, I think she was getting sort of sick of it. Normally, parents really enjoy yelling. But I guess it's like anything else—too much of a good thing, and it's not as fun anymore.

What's weird is, until this move came along, I hardly made my parents yell at all. I don't mean I am an angel or anything. But I get good grades at school, and I've never been arrested. I don't think parents can ask for much more than that.

I used to actually even *like* my parents. They had always been pretty understanding, pretty fair. They didn't go around tickling me in public or embarrassing me the way some parents do. That's what was so crazy about our "big move." They hardly even discussed it with me! I'm not kidding. My father just came home all excited one day and told me he'd gotten this big promotion and we'd be moving to Massachusetts. That was it! We didn't even take a vote!

He made it sound real cheery, of course. Whenever parents announce something you're going to hate, they try to spice it up and make it sound better than it is. They kept calling the move "a great new adventure." Then they spent a lot of time telling me how much better off I was going to be because of my father's new job.

They talked about college and my future, stuff I couldn't care less about right now. So instead of feeling better, mostly I just felt sick to my stomach.

I cried a lot after I found out. I didn't do it much in front of my parents, though. When you're ten and a half, you don't like a lot of people sitting around watching your nose run. That's why I saved most of it for my room, muffling my blubbering sounds with my pillow. Sometimes it got so soggy, I couldn't sleep on it.

I was also more scared than I'd ever been before. But it wasn't the kind of scared you feel when you think there's a dead guy with a hatchet hiding in your closet at night. It was a new kind of scared. Moving makes you feel all alone inside. You don't know what the new town is going to look like, or your new house, or your street, or even what kind of people you'll meet. It may not *sound* scary. But if you ever have to move, you'll understand what I mean.

Anyway, besides making me feel sad and scared, the whole idea of moving also made me furious. How could my parents do this to me? How could they just whisk me away from all my friends, and my school, and my soccer team, and then tell me what a "great new adventure" I was going to have? Did they actually expect me to be happy about it? Did they think that I had no feelings? That they could just pick me up like some dumb stuffed animal and set me down any old place, and I'd be fine?

As the car neared the end of my street, I started fidgeting.

"I'm bored and my leg's hot," I whined. "Also, I think I might be getting carsick."

At the wheel, I saw my father shaking his head in disgust. "Come on, Howard. Not today, okay? Why don't you take some time off from complaining and just relax?"

Relax? I thought to myself. *Are you kidding? Complaining is my job now. It's what I* do.

Suddenly my mother reached into a bag in the front seat and tossed me back an orange. She does this sort of thing a lot when we're traveling. Since I've never been what you'd call a good little traveler, my mother buys a bunch of stuff to keep me busy so I won't gripe. When you think about it, it's kind of insulting—like feeding a gorilla a bunch of bananas so he won't bother you.

I was particularly annoyed at my mother lately—especially after what I heard her say to Aunt Emily on the phone. It happened a couple of days before we moved. I was sitting on the back stairs, so she didn't know I was around.

"Yeah, he's not too happy about it right now, Em," she had said. "But you know how kids are. Once you get them there, they always seem to bounce right back."

Bounce right back! I'm not kidding. She really said that! She made me sound like a Nerf ball. Like she had a foam rubber son with no emotions at all!

The more I thought about it, the more annoyed I got. I tried to take my mind off things by looking out the window, but my father's voice distracted me.

"Hmm," he said, pondering out loud. "I wonder if the van will get to Massachusetts before we do."

The moving van! Why did he have to bring up that stupid moving van? I hated that van and all the stupid moving men that came with it! The day they packed our stuff had been the worst day of my life.

My parents were upstairs when the knock came at the door. "Answer that, would you, Howard?" called my father. "We're busy up here."

"I can't!" I called back. "I'm in my pajamas!"

My father was standing at the top of the stairs with his hands full. "No one cares what you're wearing, Howard. Just let the men inside."

"*I* care what I'm wearing! Have you seen these things? Would someone please tell Nana that I'm too old for Porky Pig pajamas?"

"Howard!"

My father was using his killing voice. You can push him so far, but when he uses his killing voice, it's best to do what he says. I went to the door.

"Hi, sonny."

There were three of them, all lined up in their

brown moving-men suits. They came inside. One of them looked at my pajamas and whistled. "Porky Pig, eh?" he asked.

I covered Porky with my hands and ran up to my room. Then I locked the door so no one could come in. Later, when the movers were ready to pack my stuff, my father got a key and opened it.

It still makes me sick when I think about it. The moving man stomped right in and started dumping all my stuff into big boxes. He just heaped it together like it was garbage or something. When the marbles fell out of my Chinese checkers, he dumped them in the box without even putting them back in the game first. It really made me furious. I don't even *like* Chinese checkers, but a guy still likes to keep his marbles together. . . .

I concentrated harder on looking out the car window. As luck would have it, we were just passing Thornsberry's house. Seeing it gave me this real empty feeling in the pit of my stomach. Barry Thornsberry is one of my best friends. Saying good-bye to him and to my other best friend, Roger Grimsley, had been the hardest thing I'd ever had to do in my whole life. The three of us practically grew up together. I know this sounds mean, but I felt closer to Thornsberry and Roger than I did to my very own baby brother. I mean, we've even known each other longer—since preschool. Our teacher, Miss Filbert, introduced us and assigned us to the same work table.

Thornsberry was crying at the time. Of the three of us, he's the most sensitive. He thought his mother had given him to Miss Filbert for keeps. It took him about a week to figure things out.

I didn't like Thornsberry at first. It's hard to get to know a kid who only talks to you from behind a Kleenex. I liked Roger, though. On the first day of school, Miss Filbert asked us to draw a picture of our family. Roger drew a cow.

"Uh, that's a very nice cow, Roger," she said. "But are you sure you understood the project? You were supposed to draw a picture of your family."

Roger just smiled happily and nodded.

Later we learned that cows were the only things Roger could draw. By the end of the year, Miss Filbert had taught him to stand them on two legs and dress them in clothes. Personally, I thought this was a big mistake. In kindergarten, every time Roger drew a picture of his family, it looked like they all had cow heads.

Before the move, I'd talked a lot of my worries over with Thornsberry and Roger. They hated my leaving almost as much as I did, but they tried to make me feel better about it.

"Come on, Howard," said Thornsberry. "Maybe it won't be as bad as you think."

"How could it not be bad?" I asked glumly. "Didn't you ever study about Massachusetts in history? The Pilgrims moved there, and by the first winter practically all of them were dead."

Roger made a face. "I hate Pilgrims. I've hated them ever since my mother made me be one on Halloween. Remember that? She made me wear that stupid top hat and long black coat. Everyone thought I was Abraham Lincoln carrying a turkey."

Thornsberry gave me a funny look. "You

don't really think you're going to *die* there, do you, Howard?"

"Well, maybe not actually *die*," I admitted. "But I'm going to have to go to a stupid new school, and that's almost like dying."

Every time I thought about it, my stomach tied itself in knots. "God, I can't believe it. I'm actually going to have to be a new kid."

Thornsberry and Roger groaned.

"We got a new kid in our room about a week ago," Roger said. "No one can remember his name, so we just call him by the color of his shirt. On Thursday he was the kid in the green shirt. On Friday he wore a shirt with his name on it, so we called him the kid in the Kenneth shirt."

Thornsberry hit Roger on the arm. "We're supposed to be making him feel better, remember?"

"It doesn't matter," I replied. "It's not like I don't know what happens to new kids. I've had enough of them in my class to see how hard it is to fit in."

"Yeah, but you won't have any trouble, Howard," said Roger. "It's not like you're a geek or anything. At school you're practically even *popular.*"

"Sure, Howard," added Roger. "You won't have any trouble. You'll see."

Thinking about how nice they had tried to be almost made me start to cry. My mother must have heard me sniffle or something, because she turned around.

"What's the matter?" she asked, raising her eyebrows sympathetically.

"Everything," I answered dismally. "Everything's the matter."

She just sighed and turned back around. A second later she threw over a granola bar.

Instead of saying thank you, I made a noise like a gorilla. She didn't say anything, but I'm pretty sure she got the message.

We had turned onto the highway by then, so I spent the next couple of hours reading signs, trying to get my mind off the move. It wasn't easy, though. Every few minutes, we'd pass a billboard with kids painted on it and I'd start wondering about the kids in Massachusetts.

What would they be like? Would they dress the same way we did in Arizona? I hoped I would fit in. One time we had a German kid visit our school, and he wore a suit and a bow tie. He looked like a little grandfather or something.

Anyway, all I've got to say is that moving really stunk. And even though it's over now, I still don't blame myself for the way I acted about it. A lot of mean stuff has been done to me—by my parents, by the moving men, and by my father's stupid company. And even though sometimes you can control your anger, you can't control your sadness. And that's what I mostly was, I guess—sad. Sad about leaving my friends and my school and my room and my soccer team and a million other things.

If you've ever been sad, *really* sad, you know what I'm talking about. Sadness is with you all the time. Even when your friends are trying to make you laugh, sadness seems to be waiting right behind your smile.

Award-winning middle-grade reads from

Barbara Park

#1 *New York Times* bestselling author of Junie B. Jones

"Barbara Park makes reading fun."
—Dav Pilkey, author of Captain Underpants

"Sheer outrageousness!"
—Andrew Clements, author of *Frindle*